The Trio

by

Diana Toups

Portions of this book are works of fiction. Any references to real events, people, or places are used fictitiously. Portions of this book are works of nonfiction. Certain names and identifying characteristics have been changed.

The Trio

ISBN: 978-1-64921-366-2

Dedicated to Mother Mary:

dreamer, lover, daughter, mother…
Palestinian Jew

"A Christian is aware that she is part of her society and of all its sufferings. She is neither a stranger nor a spectator. She lifts up in prayer discriminations, injustices, war, occupation and death, saying: 'O God, look and have mercy . . .' And amidst wars she will be a peacemaker." - Patriarch Emeritus of Jerusalem, Michel Sabbah

Mother Mary, Queen of Palestine, pray for us.

FOREWARD

Zoughbi Zoughbi

Founder of Wi'am:

The Palestinian Conflict Transformation Center

Bethlehem, The Holy Land

This heart-wrenching story depicts the Ein Karem tragedy of 1948—one of the most critical events in Palestinian history. *The Trio* captures a snapshot of the devastation that occurred during Al-Nakba or "The Catastrophe" during which over 500 Arab villages were destroyed.

1948 is characterized by terror for the Palestinians, who fled from killing, violence, and ethnic cleansing. Even today, The Nakba is ongoing in different areas of Historic Palestine where the indigenous people are still forcibly removed and new settlers take their place.

For those who did not have the privilege of visiting Palestinian villages before the Nakba, this story offers a new didactic history and spirituality, in which beauty, hope, nature, family, and animals exist in harmony. This story also baptizes hope anew. "Hope Remains!" insists Olive, the patriarchal tree, emphasizing what all Palestinians believe: we cannot lose hope.

The Trio unpacks horrifying events through dialogue, emphasizing rights, but never revenge. The familiar Palestinian story of refugees and keys is given new life, raising questions which remain pertinent today: Where is justice? Does love cast out all fear? Is it right to ask, "Why is God unfair?" At the same time, this tale reminds us that our land, the land of our Lady Queen of Palestine, is filled with blessings. Both the challenge and answer are continuously uttered: "This Land demands justice," and "Surely the burden will never outweigh the blessings."

The author, Diana Toups, came and lived in the Holy Land. She has not only put herself in the shoes of others but has walked countless miles and more within them. She has listened to the beatings of the natives' hearts. She has lived their agony, passion and suffering. Diana, in her words, has captured displaced families' ambitions, dreams and hopes. Although not born Palestinian, she shares our burden and awaits with us a better future. She speaks on behalf of the marginalized without biases or prejudice, and imbues her writing with great love, understanding, and empathy—the most powerful motivator of all.

When reading this story, Mary Anne, a refugee from Ein Karem, wept passionately. It is beyond refreshing to hear our voice through someone who cries and weeps with us, who is ready to celebrate and cherish life with us, and who is full of hope despite all odds. Diana is a modern historian who is targeting the international audience with a people's narration that goes beyond news reports and analysis, and paints the Palestinians and their culture as it is and was, with all its beauty.

Readers of this story will gain a richer, deeper, and more human understanding of the Palestinians' plight, lives and society. They will explore new breath and depth in contemplating the events, views and words of the characters in a symphony that is terrific and factual, reflecting beauty, hope and breathing . . . all forms of our resistance.

I highly recommend this story of the forcefully displaced people, who continue to demand justice, and justice alone. They are the sons and daughters of humanity, who love to celebrate life, not death, and their voices, ready to be heard, speak loudly in this beautiful narration of one of their many tragedies.

May you hear their voices, and may we together turn this tragic history into a brighter future, characterized by inclusivity and justice for all. Thank you to all who have wept and continue to weep tears with us. May our hopes be realized, and may we inclusively embrace in celebration the justice and freedom to come.

Part One
The Center of the World

Carmel was swinging near the old lemon tree in the center of the world embroidering the hem of her new party dress. As her brown fingers worked geometric shades of bright red and pink into a background of dark blue, her cat Jameela stretched out like a lazy pillow beside her on the green metal seat. Together they swayed back and forth in the dry breeze to the tinkling music of dishes and spoons as her mother, grandmother, and three of her sisters began preparations for an abundant pot of grape leaves and chicken in the kitchen. They were expecting the local priest for dinner.

And the everlasting olive tree which held the spirits of her ancestors hovered over the white entry gate, guarding the peaceful scene like a jealous patriarch.

The early May sky was dappled with transient clouds, and chickens danced to the humming of backyard hives as Carmel listened to the playful antics of four younger brothers spreading tomatoes to dry on the flat roof. The blessing of rain would not reach Palestine again until September. Her grandfather was in the orchard picking apricots which had ripened under the awning of heaven, thanks be to God, and the blossoming scent of oranges filled his lungs like the promise of a sweet tomorrow.

Round, desert-colored pots of fragrant herbs luxuriated about the pale stone courtyard like satiated house guests: mint, oregano, basil, thyme and sage. Fourteen children ranging from nineteen to none played and smiled and worked high upon the ancient terraced hill in Vineyard Springs with their parents, two grandparents, three fat cats and one scraggly dog.

And sleepy Olive, near the entry gate, nodded his head contentedly.

Carmel smiled as the sun began to set behind her grandmother's statue of Our Lady, Queen of Palestine, whose hazel eyes and outstretched arms greeted every bird and guest. The virgin's painted robes of blue and red now glowed with golden hues, outshining even the brightest oleanders on the gently sloped hillside beyond.

To seventeen-year-old Carmel, sunsets were filled with mysteries of primordial attraction. They were a soulful blend of strong opposites, a sacramental marriage of day and night.

When all light and colors magnified and blended, especially upon the sea, sometimes it was impossible to tell where the earth ended and heaven began. Sunsets were a hopeful symbol, a daily challenge to the earth of what could be.

As Carmel's world blended into a syrupy orange knaffeh, she took a deep breath, trying to capture the enchantment inside of her.

"If we watch patiently until the end," she whispered to Jameela, "we will inhale secrets to the universe."

Carmel finished her work as the magic faded and peered in through the kitchen window where many empty ceramic cups arranged on a round serving tray giddily anticipated the arrival of hot mint tea. The wide wooden family table built by her grandfather was adorned with blue and yellow bowls of zaatar, oil, olives, apricots, wild figs and early grapes. Carmel marveled at how effortlessly her charming mother could assemble an evening poised for good food and conversation.

Her mother flourished her spoon like a maestro, her directives like a song, all the while tending to the assorted needs of young children and aged parents. Carmel could hear her mother now, praying aloud as she tucked the littlest ones into bed. Three-year-old Mikhal was loudly yet sleepily protesting that he wanted to stay up for the arrival of the priest.

The priest! Where is the priest? Carmel thought. *He is never this late, not even for the earliest mass!*

As soon as the thought arrived, the scraggly grey dog, with a prelude to the answer, barked an alarm from the white entry gate. Fat Jameela sprang to the thorny cover of the lemon tree with surprising agility as Carmel's eldest brother ran home from the vineyard shouting one word, "Soldiers!"

Carmel marveled as her brother's white cotton shirt billowed about him like a parachute coaxing him to fly. In the distance, grieving church bells resounded in pain, slow and ominous with the knell of death, and her needlework slipped from her lap.

And Olive trembled to his roots, delving so deep into the land it was said he would never die.

"Why are you here?" a young soldier demanded, his accent strange and menacing. Behind him, two more soldiers pointed guns at her brother's white chest and father's brave face. "Haven't you heard? All of your neighbors in Vineyard Springs have fled. We have slain the villagers from the nearby town and razed their homes. Leave now before we destroy you as well."

Mama's head was bowed in sweet Arabic bedtime prayers as she nursed the infant son strapped to her breast and nestled three small children into their shared bed, under the quilt her mother had made, when the world changed.

Father was sitting on the brown settee in the living room, preparing a smoking pipe in anticipation of the arrival of his friend, the priest, who was never late, when the world changed.

Carmel's flowing yellow skirt caught in the unforgiving thorns of the fickle lemon tree, and she fell hard to the ground at the foot of the virgin near the courtyard well, when the world changed.

And in the center of the world, Olive drank deeply from within the current of the earth, filling the fibers of his ancient arms with the blood of catastrophe.

Part Two
Catastrophe

Carmel's family fled in panic, falling to their hands and knees in the dirt of their ancestors, stumbling through purple brambles and holy thistles with no more than they could strap to their bodies. This consisted mostly of elderly grandparents and children.

Father locked the thick wooden front door and pocketed the skeleton key as they made their way toward town. Sixteen people progressed together, alternately encouraged and frightened by the yelping assurances of Francis the dog and Carmel's mother's shrieking prayers. They escaped down the steep hillside as one misshapen body while Carmel's warm blood, like a temple offering, poured over the smooth courtyard stones her grandfather, father and brothers had laid.

And Olive, whose blessed chrism oil anoints the heads of babies as well as the hands of priests, was shaken so, that his un-ripened fruits, as if crushed in a press, burst open in the color red.

Three hours of darkness had passed when a scream that should have melted the night woke Carmel from her resting place. It was the wailing of Mikhal, her three-year-old brother, who had inadvertently been left behind in his bed. Carmel found Mikhal sobbing under his patchwork quilt that their grandmother had fashioned from her faded dresses. Yet, as hard as she tried, she could do nothing to console him. Her only option was to follow him as he wandered into the fields and cried to the point of exhaustion. Eventually she managed to bundle him up, and Mikhal slept soundly in his sister's arms under the scanty branches of an acacia until morning.

When Carmel opened her eyes, she found she had been magically returned to her white entry gate. Her house and yard had somehow separated from the town as if scooped in a measuring cup and deposited on a grocer's scale like almond and pistachio candies. Her family's swing, orchard, and courtyard now hovered a few feet in the air, resting upon a huge dish, one half of a grand, uneven scale. Yet the scale was so large, the dish on the other side could not be seen. The soldiers were gone, and three-year-old Mikhal was gone as well. Even Jameela, the beautiful cat, could not be found.

"It's the weight of injustice," Olive said, regarding the elevated house. He looked older, but also somehow stronger.

"What sort of evil reposes on the other side of this scale, Olive? Who is to blame for this catastrophe?"

"We shall see," said the tree.

And the world turned, and Olive grew wiser, and Carmel's heart grew in size and emptiness.

Ripened grapes and figs plopped to the ground like unopened missives, in the center of the world. The sweet juice of the pomegranates went to waste, and the rains came too late to infuse life into the scorched courtyard herbs. Then one day, scraggly Francis, the family dog, showed up with Carmel's father's shiny house key tied about his neck by a long, strong cord.

"Francis! It's good that you are here!" said Carmel, hugging his neck. "How are you? How is my mother?"

The dog shook his unkempt head. "Your family, save little Mikhal, live as refugees in a filthy camp just a few miles away. Your mother and father beg the army every day to allow them to return home, but they are not permitted."

If the dog could have touched Carmel's heart at that moment, he would have felt it break. "But do not worry," he announced. "I have a plan. Do you see this key?" Francis dangled her father's key before her as if it were a magic charm. "I will fasten one end of this cord around the trunk of the lemon in the courtyard above, and at my end I will sit here with the key near the white entry gate, so that when our family is allowed to return, they will always be able to find the front door."

Francis leapt effortlessly, high up onto the scale, and he did as he said. Soon he returned with the skeleton key securely tied around his neck.

And in the center of the world, Olive and the girl and the dog lived together, on the ground near the white entry gate with the key, and the cord like a kite, traveling up amongst the fruits of the lemon, awaiting their family's return.

To the trio's alarm, before the completion of six months, while the garden cabbages and radishes and carrots still awaited their picking, during the season of Christmas in fact, foreign soldiers returned, escorting a new family into Carmel's home. Overnight, the house, along with the entire village of Vineyard Springs, was hoisted so high upon half of the uneven scale, that neither could be reached with the tallest ladder.

"What is this madness?" yelped the dog, gasping for air as he dangled from the lemon tree high above. "The thieves are trying to hang me!"

Olive reached up grandly to save him. "They are immigrants looking for a better life," said Olive, removing the house key from the poor animal's neck, "victims of a worldwide war."

"My God, there's the pharmacy, the market, the bookstore, and the theater," said the dog, hopping on two legs and making obscene gestures with the other two. "They even stole the springs themselves, from which the town is named!"

The trio marveled at their house and town, now lifted far above their heads like heavy stone clouds threatening to crush them. Even the churches were unreachable.

"A better life at the expense of my family's?" said Carmel in a trembling voice. "In the home my parents and grandparents built?"

"I want to bite them," said the dog.

Olive bristled as he sensed a change in the season. Rains had come on and off for the past few weeks, and the weather had been alternately warm and cold. Just that morning, fog had covered the land, but now the fog had lifted, and it was decidedly cold. His roots searched deeper into the generative Palestinian soil as he silently mourned the passing of the time of bountiful harvests. His roots always ran deeper when it was dry.

"Soon they will move on," said Carmel, who still firmly believed in justice, "and find a place of their own."

"Perhaps," said Olive, who with the cord now stretched ridiculously thin from his ancient limbs to the home high above, did not sleep that night, nor for many nights afterward.

And in the center of the world, the full yellow moon wooed new dreamers on the ornate green swing, the traitorous lemon bore ripe fruit for new cups of tea, and new children slept under Mikhal's hand-sewn quilt of dresses.

To the trio's disbelief, all in the new family, the elderly to the young, with prams, baskets, books, shiny shoes and hats, claimed the house and the village of Vineyard Springs as if it had always been their home. The new tribe scurried to and fro as if everything was normal, hoisting their flags and eating their feasts on the wide wooden table her grandfather had built. Carmel wondered if the new family had enjoyed the dried tomatoes from the roof—and what ever happened to her embroidered blue dress?

One night, Carmel was startled awake as Francis bayed in long moans of grief. "Is it ignorance, callousness, or jealousy that would provoke such a thing? They have destroyed your grandmother's statue. This is all that's left!" The dog trotted over with the icon's open hand in his mouth and laid it at the base of the tree.

"It's fear," Carmel said as she felt the indentations in the worn fingers of Our Lady's stone hand. The stone was warm, as if the memory of her grandmother's countless petitions still lingered inside. Carmel wished the beloved relic could somehow bring her some peace. But hard as she tried, she could not summon the dimmest shred.

"Fear? I don't understand," said the dog, still panting in distress. "It is we who should be fearful."

"Because love casts out all fear," Carmel said as she placed the severed hand in the arms of the olive. It looked like an empty cradle. "They obviously don't love us. They don't even notice us."

"They fear the unknown?"

"Exactly."

"Oh my," said the dog. "Then it will be all too easy for them to hate us."

And the wizened tree who now recognized the invisible injustice weighing down the opposing side of the scale, sensed the coming of a nameless doom.

One evening just after dusk, Olive regarded the children seated around the wide wooden table, filling their little bellies with bean soup. "Have faith, dear ones," he assured his friends. "Surely their sweet children will grow to break this dark spell. Perhaps if we dance and sing . . ."

This seemed such an absurd request coming from the old tree. Carmel feared his brain had hardened. "Oh! Beloved Olive!" said Carmel as she gazed at the stars hovering mockingly beside her lost home, wondering at the provocations of the family inside. "Tell me why our glorious God, who made the heavens, who calms the seas, who causes the sun to rise and set, decided that His Son should live and teach and heal and die in the land of my great grandmother's birth? Why did our Creator, who could have hung His grace from a cloud, choose to clothe Himself in the flesh and blood and arms and milk of a Palestinian virgin? Is it a blessing or a curse? What is it here in my grandmother's homeland, that even God covets?"

The immortal tree was silent for a few moments. "It is our steadfastness, dear Carmel," he replied with certainty.

"Our steadfastness?"

"Yes, dear Carmel. Because we are a sturdy people, Palestine, our home, has been chosen to bear a great weight."

"What will happen if Palestinians weaken?" Carmel wondered.

"We shall never weaken," said the tree.

And with that, the trio in the center of the world, steadfastly, often vigorously, sometimes perfunctorily, draped themselves in handsome keffiyehs, embroidered in moods of dark and light, like an antithetical sunset. There was no fanciful indulgence in colorful nuptials in the veined scarves about their necks, but rather a more crucial symbol of resistance: a spirited pattern in black and white, like cloistered nuns and cassocked priests, characterizing the battle of their souls against the threat of permanent night.

"The keffiyeh matches your skin tones," said the tree to the dog.

And they danced the dabke that night and every night, for the next twenty-five years, singing intricate stanzas with throaty, Arabic lyrics, originating from far beneath their flesh, requiring enormous breath. . . .

You knelt in prayer, cool within the white stone cottage, your wide-open heart troubled by Beauty's delay. And yet still you loved, like a dark blue river: swiftly, deeply, openly, widely. Believing in Goodness, The Fashioner of everything: doves, dandelions, valleys, souls. And longing for Him to share your dreams.

One day he arrived, heralded by a page, and at once you recognized Him. For even in your greatest longing He filled you, joined you, knew you, completed you. And soon your love overflowed. Together. Bound as a single Word. Into the pulse of the untamed world.

Part Three
Resistance

After twenty-five years at the white entry gate, Carmel's eyes were still bright, but her vintage yellow dress was only barely so. Resistant hues peeked shyly from under her arms, the folds at her waist and inside her pockets, as if the wise color knew that to be seen meant to chance disappearing.

As Carmel reclined under Olive's shadow, resting on her elbow, lively music trickled down from her courtyard above, like an invitation to a party. She couldn't help wondering if her suitors would have seemed handsome on her father's brown living room settee, and whether her children would have been green eyed or brown. By the state of her dress, she supposed she might even have had grandchildren by now. She had always dreamed of imitating her mother by filling two church pews with her own babies.

The music increased with a clarinet and a drum, and foreign songs sprang from under a blue and white tent made out of a flag. Runaway white balloons escaped into the evening sky in bunches, like pretend clouds, and Carmel stretched her neck, wondering whether her family could see the balloons from wherever they were, and whether the balloons brought them sadness or joy. She hoped the children at least would find joy. Carmel pondered the luxury of joyfulness. Was it for everyone, or only the chosen few?

She thought of her brothers and the way they always good-naturedly pestered each other in the fields, in the market, and that last night on the roof. She thought of her mother and grandmother, how they always believed that good could come even from the greatest sorrow.

"I smell falafel," said the dog, perking up his nose. But he was not comforted. "Now the robbers have even stolen our food! The treachery is complete."

Oh! How Carmel missed her mother's falafel! The scent was calming, it smelled like home. She'd almost brought herself to smile when a tuft of burning ash landed upon her lap.

The dog cursed, then began leaping about, putting out sparks in Olive's branches. "Fire!"

"God, the one thing I hate," said the tree, shaking every leaf until he was safe. "Thank you, Francis."

The new family had begun purging Carmel's family's belongings by means of a great fire in the courtyard, and flaming remnants of Carmel's past, her most treasured memories, floated down upon her. The tree, the dog and the girl each contemplated the possible meanings of this new assault.

"They are re-writing history," remarked the tree.

"Bastards!" spat the dog.

Carmel's eyes followed the flaming bits as they fell: her mother's Bible, containing locks of hair, pressed herbs and wedding flowers. A pair of white lace baby booties, records of marriages, her baby sister's baptismal gown, which had been handed down for four generations. Her father's books, her parent's anniversary photographs, all alight and carried off by the wind, as if no one in her family had ever been born. "They are trying to erase my family itself," she said.

"Too bad they won't throw down your father's hookah," grumbled the dog, still scurrying about on damage control.

Just then, Carmel spied a little girl with golden hair, about three, peering over the courtyard wall. "Oh!" She was momentarily stunned.

"Carmel!" The dog hopped in recognition, "She's wearing the hem of your blue dress as a belt!"

The child jumped back in alarm.

"Oh," Carmel said again. "She can see us, Francis!"

Carmel and the dog stood perfectly still, as if they had been caught with their fingers stuck in the icing of a wedding cake. Carmel felt, for a brief moment, as if the girl could peer straight into her. Should she say something? Could the child hear her? Should she wave? But the moment passed as quickly as it came, and the girl ducked back into the fold of her family and the fire.

"All cowards," said the dog.

"What is this word, coward?" Olive inquired, lifting his face to the falling embers. There was no such notion in his vocabulary.

"They are all pigs," spat Francis.

"She is not a coward. She has been taught to fear," said Carmel.

Olive had heard Carmel say this before, but he struggled to fathom how a small girl could possibly fear him.

"Racists!" barked the dog with a viciousness that was new to his friends.

The fire, accompanied by songs and merriment, raged late into the night, consuming all physical evidence that Carmel's family had ever existed. Carmel felt that with every glowing, feathery parcel tugged away, a portion of the light within her soul was taken as well.

Then all was quiet. One by one the family members returned to the house, that was now darker than any night, as if all the stars in the sky had fallen.

And the immortal tree, for the first time ever, could not speak.

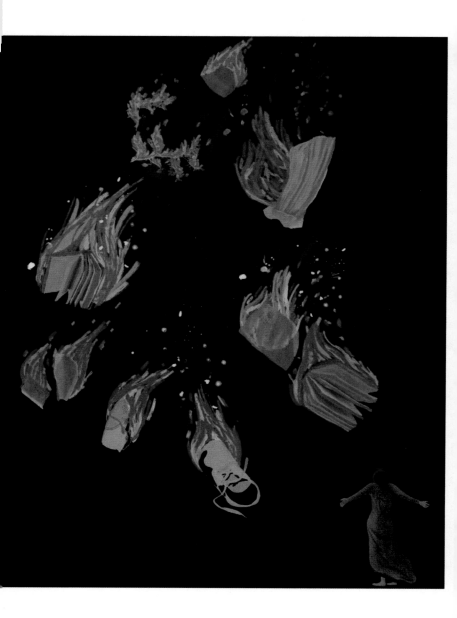

For twenty-five more years, in the center of the world, fifty years since the catastrophe, bits of letters, aromas, and shadows of Carmel's ancestors drifted among Olive's branches like dust on the wings of restless summer birds. Our Lady's hand lay like an open cup in which water sometimes collected. Carmel occasionally refreshed herself in it, with the reminder of her baptism, a reminder of her former life, and a promise of hope.

Yet the army and the resistance never rested. The catastrophe continued with increasing volume and cadence, beating like a drum from the hollow caves of the Qumran cliffs. The scale grew larger and more uneven each day, countered by a yet unseen weight. Each morning, Carmel's girlhood home and the entire village of Vineyard Springs rose higher and higher upon the elevated dish, until the accumulation of wrongs on the opposing dish grew so large it became clearly visible from the entry gate.

"Mikhal! What are you doing?" Carmel asked.

"I'm building a wall around myself and my grandchildren."

Carmel's younger brother Mikhal, to the trio's shock, grey and balding, crawled out of a new tunnel beneath the now visible dish on the opposite side of the scale. There on the dish sat a confiscated home, a ruined town, a lost childhood, but only Olive knew the true name of the doom.

"What is that stench?" asked Francis, covering his nose with his paw.

"It's death," Carmel assured him.

"Mikhal! We are so glad to see you! See? We still have the house key," said Francis, retrieving the key from Olive and trotting over to Mikhal, wagging his tail weirdly. The dog couldn't decide if he was happy or sad.

As Mikhal leaned down and petted Francis, he fingered the curves and recesses of the metal key, undoubtedly with the same wordless prayers of frustration, anger, exhaustion and faltering hope that he had offered up to a seemingly absent God for decades. "I wish it were a key to turn back time," he said.

Carmel protested with rare emotion. "We can't turn back time, Mikhal, but if you build this wall your children's children will never return to our childhood home. You are walling them off from the land, from the river, from the sea . . . forever! Why are you doing this, Mikhal?"

"It is simple. The army has commissioned me," he replied, not allowing his sister to search his eyes.

"The same army that forced us from our home?"

"Of course, Carmel, I know of no other," he said, returning the key to the dog. "But you must realize, I don't remember this home. It was ten years before I was able to leave the orphanage and join our family in the refugee camp. Imagine. I was thirteen when I discovered that the mother I had longed to see for ten years, had long ago died of a broken heart."

Carmel gasped.

"What did you think, Carmel, that just because you have

chosen to lounge here at this sentimental gate that the world would not go on without you?" Mikhal noticed the look on his sister's face. "I'm sorry, I thought you knew," he said flatly. "Look, there are mountains of such tragedies in Palestine, far too many to count. You are not unique. There are many such scales, some much larger than this. This dish you see here, this dish that is so large it has created a deformity in the earth, represents only one town, our town, Vineyard Springs. Your death is represented in that stinking pile somewhere, Carmel. What do you think of that? Your death was meaningless. It did nothing but add to a whole pile of senseless grief, and the misery grows every day. These wrongs will never be balanced."

"You mustn't say such things, Mikhal!"

"Hope remains, dear Mikhal," said Olive, stroking Carmel gently with a sheltering limb. "It is completely within the powerful army's capability to right this wrong. Come, dear Francis. I will take the key again for safekeeping."

"Agreed," said Mikhal, unperturbed by the ruminations of a talking tree. "It is within the powerful army's control, but they choose not to do it. Even if this chosen family in the sky moves out of our home, the army will never allow us to return. Where is the hope in that?"

Carmel's wide and empty heart suddenly felt as if a share of the coming wall had been poured inside, as if by this new weight she had become part of the land. "But you cannot lose hope, my brother!"

"I have to put food on my children's table, Carmel." Mikhal's head and body were bent. His eyes were aimed at the ground. "Dear sister, the land you inexorably belong to has betrayed you. She has allowed everything worth loving to be either stolen or destroyed."

Carmel knew this was not true, but still she had to force herself to search hard for an answer. "Not everything. They cannot steal our ability to love, Mikhal!"

Mikhal raised a hand to silence his sister. "Please. Just let me do my work and let's not speak of this again."

"Clearly you must be dead, Mikhal, or you would not be speaking to me at all."

"Yes, clearly, dear Carmel. My heart still beats, but my soul is dead. Do you know, my family and I live without clean drinking water in a permanent camp only a few miles away, in Bethlehem? We are despised like flies in a manger."

"I didn't . . ."

"Do you know, my thirteen-year-old grandson, Saeed, was shot by a sniper in front of me as he was returning home from school less than one year ago?" Mikhal paused to allow them time to digest the image. "Do you know, I can still feel the warmth of his blood? It mocked my fingers as I tried to close his princely heart. I can smell the lead that invaded his chest and hunted him like a phantom, greedily pursuing even his soul as it rose, lest it try to escape the occupation. Every night in my dreams, Saeed rebukes me for all the promises I foolishly made him, promises for a better life, for an education, for children of his own, for freedom. Do you know what Saeed means?"

"It means *happy*."

"Yes. You see, I named the child. Once . . . I had hope,

sister. But no longer. I should hate, but I am too tired. I wish it had been me that died instead."

Carmel saw a great angel open a vast scroll and pour onto the scale the names of all from Vineyard Springs who had died unjustly. Along with her own name, Carmel recognized that of her mother, Saeed, and the priest. The scales of inequity tipped violently with the burden of the deaths of innocents. And Carmel's home, as if escaping from the indignation, rose so high into the clouds that it was almost impossible to see from the white entry gate.

Olive groaned like timber breaking. His arms threatened to be torn from his body as he struggled to maintain his hold on the key.

And Mikhal uttered not a sound as he was knocked to his knees by the deluge of martyrs.

Oh Palestine! Let us finger the imprints hidden within your wide-open heart, so that our hearts may beat as one with yours. We have spikenard, oil, mud and mikveh. Come dance with us, cry with us, sup with us, let us listen. Share with us your songs and sighs, the desperation of your hands, the wisdom of your belly, the worn paths of your feet, the silence of your wounds.

Let us pull you in and pour our tears over your brown and wearied body. Let us dry your sandaled feet with the scented strands of our tangled hair. Let us greet your dimming eyes with the singular promise of our devotion. Let us drink of your beauty and fill our lungs and soul to over-flowing with the jagged contours of your longing: your unheard keening, your unpaid blood, that longs to be free.

Surprisingly, in the center of the world, the new family never heard the boisterous singing of the nightly dabke, which was very loud, nor the baying of the miserable dog, which was even louder. They did not seem to be bothered by the wall, although the dog often pointed out surely it could easily be seen from up there. The new family never even noticed the stain of Carmel's blood on the smooth stones beneath their feet.

"What is it Olive?" Carmel was curious as to why the tree appeared to be smiling and crying at the same time. He indeed was aging.

"It's your mother," he grinned. "You know Mikhal is wrong. She is still with us."

"Of course, she is," offered Francis. "All but the shameless can hear her nightly moaning as she hunts for her dead children just outside their bedroom windows." Carmel was either too polite or too tired to argue.

"Carmel," Olive grinned wider, "she's with us! Come lay your head at my feet. See? Just breathe. No, slowly. There now, listen. Her lilac laughter remains so pleasantly amongst my fruits. Of course, it does, she so often rested beneath my arms when she was a child. Her sweetness remains with me, even now."

Carmel laid her head at Olive's feet where she herself had read countless books nestled safely and magically within his charms and scent and height and age.

"And put your hand here, lightly. Can you feel it?" The tree was saying. "The crease of her smile still dwells where she so gracefully paused and trimmed and guided my way for so many seasons."

Carmel ran her fingers along Olive's torso where memories of children and singing and large gatherings impressed upon his bark like frets and stanzas and pages of songs. Her family's breath vibrated musically from his heart. Tousled strands of curly hair and locks of colloquies composed the laced fabric of his leaves. Carmel let out a long, contented sigh.

"See Carmel? A strong essence such as hers must endure. She is part of the world, of me, of the encircling, everlasting roots woven beneath these stones, this sky, your family, our land. She will never die."

And Carmel beheld, and listened and believed, as if the words Olive spoke held a power to make things come true.

Francis shielded his eyes with one paw, straining his neck upward. His tongue begged for respite. The entire world seemed dirty. Even the sun seemed gloomy. Their matted keffiyehs were almost a memory. He scoffed as he observed the comings and goings of the inhabitants above. "I wish I could sit in the silent library of Vineyard Springs reading tales of adventure."

"I loved that library," Carmel sighed.

"No wait, I want to bathe my boney butt in the cool springs while drinking freshly squeezed pomegranate juice from the market. Actually," he added after a short pause, "what I wouldn't give to eat a bucket of wild figs and leave a warm runny present on their doormat."

Carmel laughed. "I love you, Francis. But don't you think the family is suffering as well?"

"Suffering? Their dogs have it better than your brother."

"That may be true, Francis. But sometimes I feel sorry for them, don't you?"

"No."

"Francis, every day their children are taught to fear, even to hate the very people who built the roof over their heads. Isn't that sad?"

"I won't ever be able to bring myself to feel sorry for them, Carmel. You are obviously far holier than I," said the dog. "Because as long as they think they are the victims, there will never be peace, there will always be war and hate in this so-called holy land. I hate them, and you should too."

"Hatred is violence, sweet Francis," Carmel sighed, softly stroking between the dog's ragged ears. "I am no longer human;

I am not capable of it."

"But if you were human?" postulated the dog.

Carmel was not sure she wanted to answer this question, or even that she could. The now tarnished house key dangled jeeringly from Olive's branches. The air gasped, as if God was withholding even the comfort of rain from Palestine in order to either chasten or strengthen His people. Meanwhile, the mire from the opposing dish advanced like storm-driven waves toward the white entry gate.

"What is that new monster?" said the dog, gesturing to a fresh mound of injustices added to the huge scale.

"My God," Carmel mouthed in wide-eyed silence as the trio fought to comprehend the latest insult.

Most of them appeared to be well over a hundred years old, and yet they had engaged in a great struggle. All had been burned and hacked, and some had been ripped apart by heavy machinery. Some were painted with racist graffiti, as if loyalty to the land was an offense. Their forms were almost unrecognizable, yet even in death their dark, mutilated limbs silently reached to the sky for justice. In the strange silence was a thick, immovable dread. The dog's nostril's flared involuntarily.

"They nourished the land with their blood," observed the tree. Olive had heard about such practices, but he had never witnessed such horror. It was hundreds of olive trees, their charred bodies hacked to pieces, then piled on the scale.

"What the hell has happened to the holy land?" Francis begged.

"Perhaps a better question might be, what has happened to the holy people?" replied Carmel.

The trio sat in silence for hours that blistering day as their town and home bustled with activity above. They felt betrayed and deserted, like two-dimensional faces in a vanishing black-and-white photograph stuffed into the bottom of a cardboard box. And each of them secretly wondered if they, indeed all of Palestine, would soon disappear along with their memories.

And in the center of the world, the ancient olive mourned the death of his brothers. "I envy you," he said.

"You envy them because they are dead?" asked the dog.

"I envy you all," said the tree, "because you died well."

Part Four
Dreams

Days no longer contained color in the center of the world, as the wall began to cast a shadow over the trio at the white entry gate. Carmel could not even remember the last time she saw a sunset. Olive suffered from the lack of light, even to his roots, if that were possible, and the dog took to scribbling graffiti on the wall to ease his pain. He was becoming quite good.

"How do you spell *hummus*," Francis wanted to know, spraying the dull wall in shades of red, black and green. "Is it with one *m* or two?"

"Two," said Olive, enjoying the atypical scene. "Write this down for me please: Olive Palestine!"

And the tree and the dog shared a rare and hearty laugh in the shadow of the unnamed doom.

At the beginning of every shift, in the center of the world, Mikhal's bowed form emerged from the guarded tunnel under the opposing dish. He emptied his pockets and removed his belt, along with the last of his self-worth, in order to work on the wall, like a prostitute forced to sell his body for food.

Each evening Carmel watched as he crawled back inside, as slowly as the coming of a night with no moon, along with hundreds of other men—dark, bent and silent—each man preserving the dignity of the others by not speaking or glancing into the private shame in his neighbor's eyes. Mikhal always held the lit end of a thinly rolled cigarette before him, as if the subtle glow might guide his path, or as if filling his insides with fire would rid him of his loathing.

"Why do all Palestinians smoke?" wondered Carmel.

"Because all Palestinians want something to burn," answered the dog.

And the ancient tree, like a father, a brother, a worker, a friend, one who knows all and carries the joys as well as the burdens of all, was silent, alone, inside of himself with his thoughts.

"Hi," said a small voice in the darkness.

Olive turned his attention to a blond girl, about age ten, sliding down the charred remains on the dish as if they were a hill of grass. Two long braids tied with two impressive blue bows danced about her head like twin dragonflies.

"What brings you here, little one?"

"The bus," she said simply.

Olive understood. His roots felt a sudden twinge as if the very earth contracted around them. "Are you alone?"

"My mother is looking for me."

"Please, tell me."

The girl replied matter-of-factly, as if she were delivering a school report. "The blast was louder than anything I've ever heard. My body remained mostly whole," she said proudly, "but I have a scar here, see?" She showed him her arm that had been nearly severed at the elbow. "I saw the white of my mother's dress peeking like a treasure from behind shiny glass and metal. It was speckled with red and pink like the flowers in my grandmother's garden. But when I approached her, I noticed her head sat at a strange angle, and her eyes were open. When they found me wandering in the street, I was still holding on to her hand."

"Why did you come here, my child?"

The girl answered quickly, "Oh, because I saw you. I used to hear you singing from my bedroom, almost every night. See? That's my window up there," she said, pointing to the house in the air. "But when I looked out into the darkness, I could never find you. Tonight I saw you for the first time."

"Well that is something," said the tree.

The girl nodded distractedly. "Someone's coming. I hope you keep singing," she said as she and her blue dragonfly bows disappeared into the night.

Olive regarded the source of her fright. A point of red light hovered for an instant near the wall, over the dish, like a reluctant star, before disappearing. It was Mikhal passing through the tunnel to his refugee home for the last time, leaving uneven chunks of his humanity sloppily embedded into the wall behind him.

"It is finished," he said.

Guards soon filled the weaponized towers with artificial yellow light, and the metal gates banged shut, imprisoning Mikhal, the heart of her family, and millions of others on the unseen side.

And some said the violence in the land seemed to cease. The ancient Olive, like a good shepherd, standing firm between the taunting heavens and the unreachable valleys, wondered if soon the Palestinians, now enclosed within the confines of the wall, like folded sheep, would become an acceptable offering.

"Did you lie to me because I was young, Olive?" Carmel shouted.

"I never lied." The tree opened his heavy eyes like thick slices of sticky dates.

"You told me that God chose Palestine because of our steadfastness."

"He did."

"But my own brother has given up."

"He has not given up my child," wheezed old Olive, patting himself down as if searching for a lost pack of cigarettes.

"How can you say that? He's built his own prison. What on earth are you doing?"

Olive stopped massaging his old limbs and smiled as if he had just thought of something funny. "He has not given up, Carmel, because he is still breathing. In Palestine, breathing is resistance. That's pretty good, actually. I should have Francis write that down."

And that night Olive indulged in a pleasure he had denied himself for many, many years. He allowed himself to dream.

I wonder, dear Mikhal, if living, sometimes, is simply about breathing. Breathing in and out. Breathing past joys and sufferings. Waiting for Perfect Love. Waiting for human compassion to greet us. For our lives to matter. For something better.

Breathe Mikhal! Breathe in through the strong tapestry of your storied life, and breathe out as you share the steady rhythm and pulse of your existence. Breathe over tear gas and tanks, over settlements and walls, over years of injustice, with the constant gift and flow of your life force. Breathe with dancing and stars.

Perhaps, my beloved brother, one evening, when your occupiers close their restless eyes . . . a single sigh will alight upon their cheeks at night. And they will realize that it is not a knife at their throats, as their fears would have them imagine. Rather, it is that we all desire the same things. We all breathe the same air.

Part Five
Sumud

Twenty-five more years passed, in the center of the world, almost seventy-five years since the catastrophe, and the trio remained steadfast near the white entry gate. The sky appeared serene, but the western winds had failed, and the heat was awful.

Carmel, a daughter of the land, often wondered why the sky was such a poor gauge for the unhappiness of the people below. She was certain that the sky was generally unmoved by the land's misery. The sky often seemed too calm and too detached when calamity befell the earth. She wondered if the sky was too high and dignified to comment upon the terror on the ground. Maybe the sky favored the people of the sky, the people in her house, or maybe the sky was steadfast, just like herself.

She liked that last thought—that maybe, just maybe, the sky's mood was typically serene because the sky knew everything would one day turn out okay.

"Think you could reach up and get me some of those juicy peaches from that filthy family's orchard?" said the dog lazily, barely lifting his nose from the sand.

"Or honey from those sticky hives," added Carmel dreamily.

Olive chortled. He seemed lost in thought as the trio

quaked like wooden marionettes to the whining of the long, taut cord, still tied to the traitorous lemon tree in the air.

"The music of that infernal string reminds me of that silly fat cat," said the dog, lifting one ear to the awful, undulating note.

"Jameela? I have not thought of her in ages," said Carmel.

"Yes," said the dog, "the way she used to whine so creepily at night. I hated it."

"I was thinking," rasped Olive, whose verdant leaves had turned mostly silver, "the cord sounds like the wailing of poor three-year-old Mikhal left behind in his bed."

Carmel was wistful. "It reminds me of my mother's screeching prayers that same day."

The trio agreed, yes, it did.

"Do you know what I wish?" said the dog. The other two were afraid to guess, so they allowed him room to elaborate. "I wish that hideous whining was the sound of a huge missile coming to blow us all up. I am sick of being a placeholder in this land, waiting for something better, waiting for justice. I am sick of violence, of being angry, of feeling like no one cares about us at all. I despise my life. I wish the house and the land and that hateful string and this stupid gate and everything around us, even the damn house key would cease to exist. If we were all blown to bits, at least the occupation would be over, and we would be at peace."

And Carmel and Olive each felt their bodies bow in silent agreement as if something beyond them recognized this desire—not as shocking—but as somehow ugly and worthy at the same time.

No further words were spoken, but the dog's admission formed a bond between them, an uncomfortable yet permanent union of the raw, silent, horrible, eerily pleasant, desire for erasure.

Olive's fruits came into season as always, commissioned by an ageless pulse with a preternatural will to be seen, to be heard. "The house is nearing the sun," he remarked as if ordering breakfast.

His limbs bobbed and swayed under the bounty as if to a comical three-quarter waltz. To Carmel he looked overburdened and vulnerable, as if the weight of the morning dew shimmering about his leaves might break him.

"You have got some deep roots, there, brother," the dog said as he munched on a few fat green olives. When one fell from his stuffed mouth it was instantly claimed by an advancing wave from the putrid dish. "Careful where you step, Carmel. You'll ruin your dress."

"Very funny, my friend." Carmel thought she smelled smoke. She looked around for workers, but of course there were none. The wall had been complete for almost twenty years.

"Maybe it's tear gas," sniffed the dog.

A thick fog soon reached their lungs that was so heavy they struggled to breathe. But Carmel's head was as clear as the day in May when the soldiers first came to Vineyard Springs. She traveled back over seventy-five years to a joyful occasion, the feast of Our Lady of Palestine, which was celebrated every fall with rich clouds of incense, sending petitions of the local townspeople to heaven in long processions.

The perfumed smoke reminded Carmel of something she had forgotten. Was it steaming water slowly poured from her mother's tea kettle into small, welcoming blue and yellow cups?

As the aroma of incense grew stronger, the barrenness inside of her swelled like a thickened darkness, aching to be filled with the secret treasures of the universe—a beautiful, fat cat, long lost to time, a favorite cooking pot connected to multiple generations with the same spoons and recipes, a quilt of old dresses with a small needle-prick stain of her grandmother's blood in the bottom right corner.

"Be brave," said the tree. "The burden will never outweigh the blessing."

The shiver that had claimed Carmel upon the arrival of the soldiers so many years ago now returned to her body in exactly the same manner. "Olive!" she shouted. The tree had lit with a flame so sudden and so intense—nothing could be done to save him.

"That is going to demand one hell of a blessing," said the dog.

Olive's limbs hissed as his living branches were consumed by fire. His eyes closed, and he moaned as his trusty keffiyeh was no more. The cord to the house lit like a slender wick, and within seconds, their decades-old connection was severed.

Olive would have preferred to make no sound at the end, but it was not a serene passing. Still, it was dignified. Carmel stood in awe at the images that danced in the light of the fire. It was her mother and father, her grandparents, her great grandparents, all of her siblings, and people she never knew. They were crying, rejoicing, reading, sleeping, eating, smoking, singing.

"Damn, the old fossil really did hold the spirits of your ancestors," whispered Francis.

"I think they are his memories."

As the fire completely used him, Olive's plump fruits burst, rather joyfully, or so Francis thought. Thick oil flowed from Olive's outstretched limbs as if from a great chalice, down his broad back, into his everlasting roots, and deep into the battered land. Stolen homes, burned memories, destroyed villages, senseless deaths, severed limbs—all were anointed, satiating the hungry earth with centuries of loyalty until even the passive sky seemed to blush.

And then, as if in solemn observance of Olive's passing, the house in the air, although no longer connected to the key, descended a bit closer to the earth.

As smoky tendrils wafted past the house, Carmel wondered what would happen to her family now. Could Olive's gift reach Mikhal's children's children on the other side of the wall, in their colorless prison? How many generations would be born and live and die binding their subjugated necks with strings and metal keys, hurling inherited stones at barricades and armored flesh, or painting vibrant dreams upon dull walls in interminable defeat?

Would her nieces and nephews ever learn to swim in the blue-green sea? Or sink their brown toes in the muddy banks of the river?

"Now we finally know the true weight of the injustice that covers the other side of the scale," Carmel announced.

"Of course we do. It's the army and those assholes in our house, Carmel." Francis was too sad to bare his teeth.

"Yes, but not entirely, Francis."

"Please enlighten me," he said, wiping his eyes with his threadbare keffiyeh. "I'm handsome, but I'm only a dog. Why the hell is my best friend a campfire?"

Olive's trunk was smoldering, and his arms had fallen to the ground about him in a protective circle.

Carmel shook her head. "I don't know. I'm positive it wasn't his hope that burned out."

"Maybe his damn, everlasting roots finally penetrated the earth's fiery belly and did him in," Francis sniffed.

"I think it's the weight of the world."

"That explains exactly nothing, Carmel," he howled.

Carmel noticed that the opposing dish of injustices had also risen in equal measure to the house's descent. The two sides of the scale were a bit more balanced, and she smiled for the first time in a long while. It was not a smile of happiness, but one more like hope.

"Just as prayers linger in sunsets and statues, Francis, the tragedies in Palestine are related to great human tragedies that shook the earth so deeply that the air and the stones and the sand here still remember. The land still grieves, Francis. Palestine holds memories so pitiful . . . even if the people here forget, even if the whole world forgets, the very dust in Palestine cannot forget. This land refuses to rest because this land demands justice."

Olive whispered unintelligibly, resembling nothing more

than a pile of glowing coals. In the center was Mary's open, severed hand, blackened yet still welcoming like a cradle. It held the now useless house key. Carmel wished she could curl up inside it and sleep.

"You are saying the land caused this disaster?"

"Not exactly. But the land suffers so intensely, Francis. It naturally affects everything it touches. Palestinians are so innately connected to their homeland; we inescapably suffer in solidarity with her."

"God, you are telling me his sumud did him in?"

"His sumud made him worthy."

"But how, Carmen?"

"Francis, I don't know all of the answers, but Olive loved Palestine more honestly and knew her more intimately than any of us. He suffered more intensely because of his love for her. I think, out of love, he offered himself, the oil of his fruits, to heal her wounds."

"Shut your mouth, girl. That old shrub would never have given up."

"I'm not saying he gave up, Francis. I'm saying he died well."

And the girl and the dog, despite the heat of the embers, felt the world grow a little more distant, a little more cold, and a little more silent.

The dog looked over to the fading graffiti on the wall "But, Carmel! Shame on the land for accepting! It must have been a mob of those crazy tree killers!" He bristled at the memory of the mutilated olive grove on the scale.

Carmel's heart was crying with no outlet for the pain. She needed to name the doom which Olive had sheltered for so long. "Do you want to know the worst part?"

"What could possibly be worse, Carmel? That your grandchildren will also be the victims of injustice and racism? Oh wait"—the dog spat bitterly into the coals—"you will never have children, let alone grandchildren."

"Worse."

"Murder?" replied the dog, unable to tear his eyes from Olive's remains. "What could be worse than murder?"

"Indifference."

"Seriously, Carmel?"

"Yes, Francis, indifference." Carmel's voice squeaked as if her vocal cords protested saying the word out loud. "It's the scariest thing in the world."

"Why?" the dog asked in a long, almost imperceptible cry—to the embers, to the house, to the wall, to the world.

"Think about it, Francis. Indifference is lukewarm yet comfortable. It's tasteless yet satisfying. It's stagnant yet somehow fiercely unmovable. It's a destructive tolerance masquerading as something calm, safe, desirable, even luxurious. Indifference allows Palestinians, the people chosen to bear the bulk of the world's misery, to remain steadfast, here in the center, praying for freedom and peace, enduring the just demands of the keening earth, ministering to her many wounds with the ointment of our suffering, even the blood of our children, while the rest of humanity forgets."

"But, why, Carmel?" the dog asked again, in a way that begged the universe to answer.

She could hardly say the words aloud. "Because it's easier." Carmel hung her head. Her keffiyeh resembled a large, grey tear rolling down her neck.

"Easier . . ." The dog bayed in a long low moan.

"Yes. Easier. It's easier for people to forget about Palestine than to help us fight for our freedom."

As Carmel spoke these words, her eyes darkened. She exhaled slowly, the act seeming to take forever, as if releasing every moment of her long life in a single breath. She shrank into the silence that followed, bent and weathered, the dog like a statue beside her until it seemed neither would ever move again. Then, impossibly, she *breathed*.

Carmel inhaled deeply of Olive's flavor, his robust heart. She flexed her bare feet, immersed in his wizened oils, anointed by the chrism of his life. She long ago had sensed that the theft of her home, the incredible weight of violence, fear and death, had pinned her to the land longer than is customary. Now, as if rewarded for her years of steadfastness, she felt suddenly favored, like an honored wedding guest, called forth to receive Olive's standard. She spread her arms wide to welcome him fully.

Slowly, from the holy ground, traveling upward through her

body she felt new life enter her, like a child, a friend, a lover. *He filled her, joined her, knew her, completed her . . .* She sensed his memories, his fruit, his roots grip her in solidarity, oneness. *We have spikenard, oil, mud and mikveh . . .*

As gently as a sunrise, her outstretched palms became veined spring leaves, her legs rooted trunks, her hair thickened branches. Her nostrils flared slightly with heightened awareness, and her eyes closed and yet remained open, as if the veil of knowing and unknowing had been lifted. She and Olive and the land were one.

Carmel sensed but could not see the spirits of the dead, and all the joys and miseries of Palestine as well. She had become a sentinel, a watcher. She would never truly rest until the injustices in Palestine, the land of her ancestors' birth had been fully repaired. She sighed resolutely, and as she did, she felt the land's embrace. And so, with sumud, with Olive and the spirits of her ancestors, Carmel stood.

"Oh, Carmel! Carmel!" the wide-eyed dog was shouting. "If Olive knew this truth, why did he keep it a secret for so long? Why didn't he tell the world? Why didn't he tell them so they could help us?"

"Because the world wasn't ready."

"Are they ready now?"

"We shall see."

That night the two friends added new verses to their song:

Oh! Palestine! Perhaps, when we have reclined for two thousand years at your graffitied table, entered fully under the occupied cadence of your days and nights, we may discover the answer our hearts have been seeking.

Oh! Mother Mary! Somewhere within the secret of your yes . . . through the wide-open heart of your womb, beneath the easy folds of your mantle, like the forgotten house keys of Vineyard Springs, is the key to peace in God's homeland.

Oh! Lady, Queen of Palestine! Help us to repair your veil that has been split in two like the temple curtain. Is it your ancestral blood that inextricably binds our manifold wounds? Show us the heart of your homeland—the heart of your Son!

O Merciful God, like the paradox of death and redemption upon Calvary, reward our steadfast and broken hearts, by Your own design, with the simple observance of the sleeping world, and help bring our peaceful dreams to life.

The Author

Diana is a lover of both faith and reason. She is inspired by ordinary people who motivate without words, and small events that guide her heart. She is in search of messages that can be found in the quiet grandeur of nature, the mystery of coincidence, and the remarkable eyes of another soul.

She has been a wife for thirty-four years, a mother for twenty-eight, and a teacher for most of it. She hopes to be a learner forever. She is guided by the sure knowledge that we are all connected by the same powers of truth, beauty and goodness, and that love is the most powerful force in the world. She is a strong promoter of peace and justice, particularly regarding the situation in the holy land.

All proceeds from this work are directed to Bridges for Bethlehem, a US registered not-for-profit public charity supporting the poorest of the poor in Bethlehem and her surrounding areas. As Saint Mother Teresa wrote: "I alone cannot change the world, but I can cast a stone across the waters to create many ripples."

bridgesforbethlehem.com

The Illustrator

Kassidy is an adventurer, photographer and illustrator. She is an empath interested in using human connection and art to heal brokenness and share one another's stories. She is inspired by the colors in nature and the resiliency of human souls. She earned a bachelor's degree in Pre-Professional Biology from the University of West Florida in 2017. She believes that graceful approaches have the power to make lasting impacts and seeks to share the truth alongside love above all else. In her downtime, you can find her in her favorite place to be, on a mountain.

Made in the USA
Middletown, DE
08 February 2021

32954899R00044